The Miracle:The leap of faith

Sharada Shreesha

Table of contents

Introduction-5-6

Character sketches 7-11

Chapter 1 The confusion -12-14

Chapter 2 -The survival -15-17

Chapter 3 –The mysterious man- 18-20

Chapter 4-The intent 21-25

Chapter 5 –The happening 26-28

Chapter 6-The change- 29-31

Conclusion-32-37

Conclusion :Poem on Faith- 38-42

Bio-43

Introduction-

The story revolves around Raj a 25 year old boy. He is depressed at the beginning but life has another way of changing him through an incident which changes his him and his outlook towards life

Character sketches

Raj:Raj is tall.He has black eyes,black hair.He was very shabby clothes.But later on he is a transformed boy both physically and behaviorally and mentally.

Raj's mental state: Raj feels low all the time. He feels sad and he feels he is upto no good. He feels he can't do anything as he has lost interest in everything

The mysterious man

He is a tall man. He is a fairly looking man. He is in 40's. He wears dark clothes and wears a black mask.

He is charming in his talk but he has other intentions.

CHAPTER 1: THE CONFUSION

Raj: I don't know what to do with my life. I feel sad all the time. I can't concentrate on anything.

Raj: I don't feel like eating

Raj: I don't feel like sleeping, as a result I feel tired the next day.

Raj :I cannot do anything!I feel sleepy even at work.

Chapter 2 :The survival.

Raj became desperate to survive. He wasn't working. He wasn't working. Where did he have all the money. He was stealing food at the restaurant.

Raj: I am just going to pick this up without paying.

Raj even started stealing food at vegetable shops.

Raj's burglary even started to spread in the news.

Chapter 3: The mysterious man.

The man -I have to take the people here as refuge.

Raj in his unusual alertness observed the boy doing some suspicious activity in the bathroom. He was preparing threads, keeping plaster.

Raj:I have to dispose them.

The man upon realizing decided to take the newspersons hostage.

Chapter 4 :The intent:

What was the intent of the mysterious man? .Weren't we curious to know?Yes of course.

The man did not have a smooth background in his childhood. He was neglected in his childhood. He had no friends. He refused to mix with others.

Internal motive: The main was working for an external agency in his home country (eravia – imaginary country) where they were finding means to take ransom.

What were they doing with the ransom?

They were doing the ransom which they were

using it for their underdealings.

Chapter 5:The happening

Raj:Leave them and take me instead.

Raj quickly tied up the man with the ropes and reported it to the police,media.The man was held up and sent back to the country.

Raj was overjoyed that he

had come to help in some way.

Chapter 6 :The change

There were changes in Raj's life now. He was a changed person.

He was eating,sleeping,w working better too .

He was feeling better .Now he had a purpose in life.He was happier,more confident and had faith in himself.

He had belief and now he did things with belief.

He was feeling good inside and out.

Conclusion:

Faith in yourself is the key and never give up hope. Why do you think faith is important.

Faith is like a fuel which keeps

us going.Faith shows us that there is light at the end of the tunnel.Faith shows us that when we wake up we have something to look forward everyday.

What happens when this fuel within us is gone?

We become like Raj .We are unable to do

anything .We think low of ourselves and we have an inferiority complex which acts like a barrier for us to do things.

It is important for us to always hold on to some faith,belief and some optimism that everything will be okay as we may not have situations like Raj to fuel us to have faith in ourself.

Faith: A poem

Faith-The underlying message of the book.

You cannot see, feel or experience happiness in what you do. What do you do? Have faith

We feel we are inferior to others

.What do you do ? Have faith.

We feel we are different or to meak to do anything .What do we do?Have faith.

Faith is like an inner voice that there is something good coming for us. There is some higher power looking after us. All we got to do is hang on,keep trying,keep it going.

Bio- I am a curious writer interested in writing genres which also motivational in nature.

Lightning Source UK Ltd.
Milton Keynes UK
UKHW010926010922
408166UK00003B/321